PITSPOPANY

NEW YORK   JERUSALEM

MR. MENTCH

by The Mamas
Illustrated by Iosi Salem

A message from the Mamas:

To all the wonderful parents out there:-
All our children are precious and unique.
It is our job as parents to help them find
their special gift.

"Every person has to know and understand that
within them a candle burns.
There are no two candles alike ...
It is one's duty to create a flame that
will light up the whole world"
Rav Kook

Mr Mentch is just a little fish.
There's nothing extraordinary about him.
He's not a very good eater, he's not very clever
and he's not very strong.

But, Mr Mentch is a very special fish and you're **about to see why...**

Last Sunday he went to visit his friend Mr Shlemiel.

Mr Shlemiel was painting his house.
He was climbing the ladder and, in his
usual shlemiely fashion Mr Shlemiel slipped **OOPS!**

He was caught on a hook hanging by his **shoelace.**

"Oy vayzmir, Mr Mentch!
What am I going to do now?"
howled poor Mr Shlemiel.

SUPER COLOR

Just then, a school of young girl fish came swimming

"Oh nebach!" one of them said.
"Look at him! He's hanging by his shoelace!"

Mr Shlemiel looked so funny,
the girls couldn't help laughing.

super COLOR

Luckily Mr Mentch was there.
He bravely climbed the ladder, unhooked
his friend and helped him down.

"Thank you for saving me," said Mr Shlemiel,
"I don't know how that happened?"

"Achh forget it. It could happen to any fish,"
said Mr Mentch and off he swam, **only...**

He helped Dr Shmootz clean the spaghetti that was twisted around his stethoscope.

He helped Big Fress who was tangled in Zetz the octopus's tentacles.

Tuesday was the last night of Chanukah.
And the last night of Chanukah means SHOWTIME in Yiddelseas!

Excitement was in the air as fish were busy practicing their performances for the show.
Mr Mentch sat sadly watching everyone else rehearse.

Disappointed that he had no special part in the Chanukah Show,
Mr Mentch sat with his fins on his head.

"Oy yoy yoy! What do we have here?" asked Mrs Klutz,
tripping over Mr Mentch's shoe. "You look miserable!" she said.

"I feel miserable," answered Mr Mentch sadly.
"Every fish has something to do in the Chanukah show except me."

"Mmmm... I guess that is a reason to feel miserable," agreed Mrs Klutz. "So, what are you going to do about it?"

"I don't know," replied Mr Mentch.

"Tell me one thing you do well," said Mrs Klutz.

"I don't know," he said.

"What do you enjoy?" she asked.

"I DON'T KNOW!" he screamed.

"Well, I have a secret to tell you: If you can discover what you really enjoy doing, the chances are, you'll be very good at it. It's called **your special gift from Hashem.**"

And off Mrs Klutz swam right into ... guess who...?

He quickly jumped up and off he went to ...

HELP OTHERS

He rushed to help Big Fress
tune the microphone
for his rap song.

He cleaned the shmootz
off Dr Shmootz's black hat
needed for his magic act.

After the show everyone waited to hear who would be chosen as the Maccabee winner for the best Chanukah performance. Judge Chocham, the wisest fish in Yiddelseas, got up to speak. "Today, was the best Chanukah show Yiddelseas has ever seen

"Mazaltov, Mazaltov!" Shouted all the fish. They were delighted for their friend Mr Mentch who had helped them so much.

Mr Mentch jumped and jumped for joy.
He had won the Maccabee trophy and had
finally found his special gift.

GLOSSARY

Chanukah: The Jewish festival celebrating the military and spiritual victory of the Jews lead by the Maccabees in a fight for religious freedom and survival. Today, it is customary to light the Chanukiah for 8 days. We celebrate with parties, games and gifts for children. It is traditional to eat potato latkas (pancakes) and donuts.

Chocham: A wise, learned individual. The Rabbi of a community usually is one. The local ignoramus usually thinks he's one!

Fress: (fresser – noun). To eat a lot and very quickly! "I cooked for an army and the fresser ate the whole lot!"

Gantza: Entire, complete. "She ate the gantza cake and wonders why she's overweight!"

Klutz: Clumsy, awkward, graceless. "That Klutz took up ice skating? She'll be lucky if she doesn't break her neck!"

Mama: Make no mistake we mean a Jewish mother. Obsessed with food, warmth, education and healthy dose of guilt. Heaven forbid any of her children should be anything less than mentchen!

Mentch: An upright, honorable, decent person. "Now there's a real Mentch, perfect for my grand-daughter."

Oy! Oy Yoy Yoy! Oy Vayzmir! Oy Gevalt! All end with an exclamation mark!
Oy! in any form is not a word – it is an expression of grief:
Irritation – "Oy! he annoyed me"
Pain – "Oy a yoy! This pain is killing me"
Dismay – "Oy gevalt! She gained 20 pounds!"
Regret – "Oy! Did you have to invite him?"
Horror – "Oy! What? He's not Jewish!"

Plotz: To burst, explode. "If you make me laugh anymore, I'm going to plotz!"

Shlemiel: Pronounced shleh-meal, a constantly unlucky, clumsy person. He is the type to trip over his own shoelace and knock over the $1000 vase!

Shmootz: Dirt or untidy! "No matter how many times I clean the house it still looks shmootzadik!"

Yenta: A gossiper, a walking talking National Enquirer.

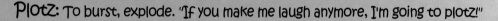
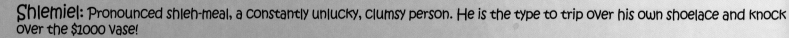